Green Light Readers
For the new reader who's ready to GO!

Amazing adventures await every young child who is eager to read.

Green Light Readers encourage children to explore, to imagine, and to grow through books. Created for beginning readers at two levels of skill, these lively illustrated stories have been carefully developed to reinforce reading basics taught at school and to make reading a fun and rewarding experience for children and grown-ups to share outside the classroom.

The grades and ages within each skill level are general guidelines only, and books included in both levels may feature any or all of the bulleted characteristics. When choosing a book for a new reader, remember that every child progresses at his or her own pace—be patient and supportive as the magic of reading takes hold.

1 Buckle up!
Kindergarten–Grade 1: Developing reading skills, ages 5–7
- Short, simple stories • Fully illustrated • Familiar objects and situations
- Playful rhythms • Spoken language patterns of children
- Rhymes and repeated phrases • Strong link between text and art

❷ Start the engine!
Grades 1–2: Reading with help, ages 6–8
- Longer stories, including nonfiction • Short chapters
- Generously illustrated • Less-familiar situations
- More fully developed characters • Creative language, including dialogue
- More subtle link between text and art

Green Light Readers incorporate characteristics detailed in the Reading Recovery model used by educators to assess the readability of texts through the end of first grade. Guidelines for reading levels for these readers have been developed with assistance from Mary Lou Meerson. An educational consultant, Ms. Meerson has been a classroom teacher, a language arts coordinator, an elementary school principal, and a university professor.

Published in collaboration with Harcourt School Publishers

Boots for Beth

Alex Moran

Illustrated by Lisa Campbell Ernst

Green Light Readers
Harcourt, Inc.
San Diego   New York   London

Requests for permission to make copies of any part of the work should be
mailed to the following address: Permissions Department, Harcourt, Inc.,
6277 Sea Harbor Drive, Orlando, Florida 32887-6777.

www.harcourt.com

First Green Light Readers edition 2002
Green Light Readers is a trademark of Harcourt, Inc.,
registered in the United States of America and/or other jurisdictions.

Library of Congress Cataloging-in-Publication Data
Moran, Alex.
Boots for Beth/written by Alex Moran; illustrated by Lisa Campbell Ernst.
p.   cm.
"Green Light Readers."
Summary: When Beth the pig's favorite boots become too small,
her friends help her find the perfect new pair.
[1. Boots—Fiction. 2. Pigs—Fiction. 3. Animals—Fiction.]
I. Title. II. Series.
PZ7.M788193Bo 2002
[E]—dc21   2001002417
ISBN 0-15-216558-4
ISBN 0-15-216546-0 (pb)

A C E G H F D B
A C E G H F D B (pb)

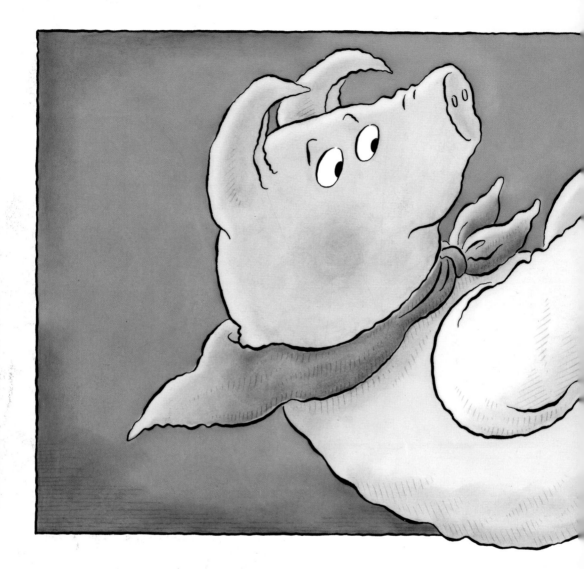

Beth was sad.

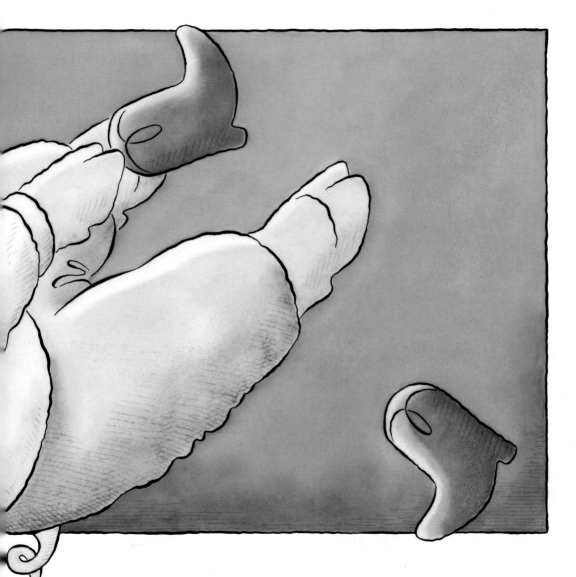

"My red boots don't fit," she cried.
"I cannot get them on."

"Could you use my boots?" asked Meg.

"Too big," said Beth.

"Will my boots fit?" asked Ned.

"Too small," said Beth.

"Could you use my boots?" asked Liz.

"Too soft," said Beth.

"Will my boots help?" asked Ted.

"Too wet," said Beth.

"Can you put on my boot?" asked Jeff.

"Too thin," said Beth.

Beth still felt sad.
Her friends all felt bad.

Then they found a big
surprise for Beth.

"New red boots!" said Beth.
"Thanks."

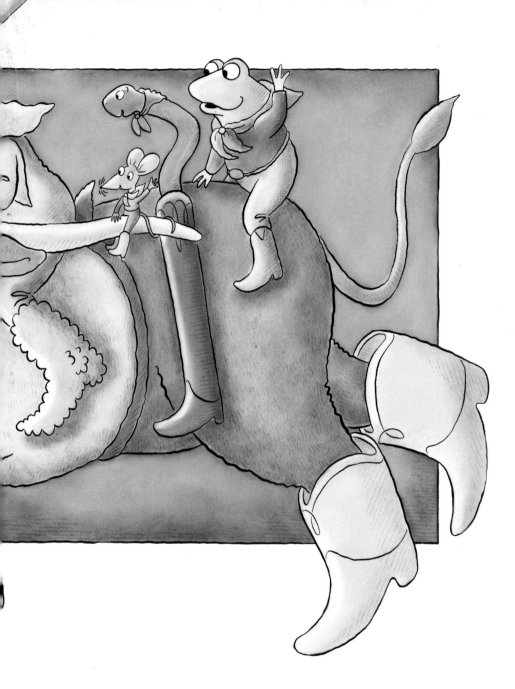

"Now, it's time to play!"
said Beth's friends.

Meet the Illustrator

Lisa Campbell Ernst got the idea for **Boots for Beth** *while shopping for shoes with her two children.* "How sad we feel when a favorite pair of shoes no longer fits!" *she says.* "Then the search for just the right new pair begins. Some shoes are too big, too small, too stiff. At last you find just the right ones!"

© Vedros & Associates

lisa Campbell Ernst